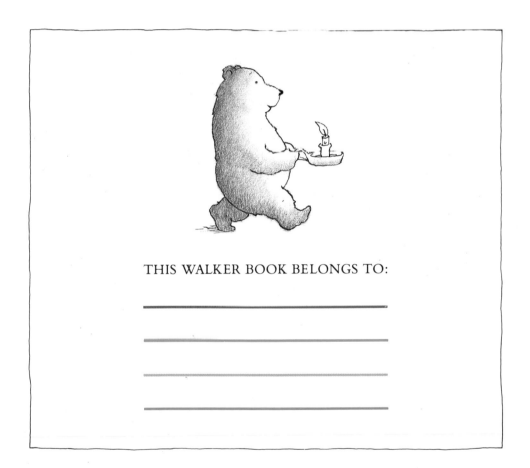

THIS WALKER BOOK BELONGS TO:

_____

_____

_____

_____

♪ ...with a little help from my friends. ♪

For Geoff, Sue, Abby, Hannah, Nick & Polly, with love. ♪

First published 1986 by Walker Books Ltd
87 Vauxhall Walk, London SE11 5HJ

This edition published 1988
Reprinted 1988 (four times), 1989

Printed in Italy by L.E.G.O., Vicenza

British Library Cataloguing in Publication Data
Murphy, Jill
Five minutes' peace.
I. Title
823'.914[J]   PZ7
ISBN 0-7445-0918-1

Five Minutes' Peace

Jill Murphy

WALKER BOOKS
LONDON

The children were having breakfast.
This was not a pleasant sight.

Mrs Large took a tray from the cupboard.
She set it with a teapot, a milk jug, her
favourite cup and saucer, a plate of
marmalade toast and a leftover cake
from yesterday. She stuffed the morning
paper into her pocket and sneaked off
towards the door.

'Where are you going with that tray, Mum?' asked Laura.

'To the bathroom,' said Mrs Large.

'Why?' asked the other two children.

'Because I want five minutes' peace from *you* lot,' said Mrs Large.

'That's why.'

Mrs Large ran a deep, hot bath.
She emptied half a bottle of bath-foam into
the water, plonked on her bath-hat and got in.
She poured herself a cup of tea and lay back
with her eyes closed.
It was heaven.

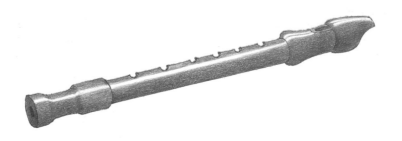

'Can I play you my tune?' asked Lester.

Mrs Large opened one eye. 'Must you?' she asked.

'I've been practising,' said Lester. 'You told me to.
Can I? Please, just for *one* minute.'

'Go *on* then,' sighed Mrs Large.

So Lester played. He played 'Twinkle, Twinkle,
Little Star' three and a half times.

In came Laura. 'Can I read you a page from
my reading book?' she asked.

'*No*, Laura,' said Mrs Large. 'Go on, *all* of you,
off downstairs.'

'You let Lester play his tune,' said Laura.

'I heard. You like him better than me. It's not fair.'

'Oh, don't be silly, Laura,' said Mrs Large.

'Go *on* then. Just *one* page.'

So Laura read. She read four and a half pages
of 'Little Red Riding Hood'.

In came the little one with a trunkful of toys.
'For *you*!' he beamed, flinging them all
into the bath water.
'Thank you, dear,' said Mrs Large weakly.

'Can I see the cartoons in the paper?' asked Laura.

'Can I have the cake?' asked Lester.

'Can I get in with you?' asked the little one.

Mrs Large groaned.

In the end they *all* got in. The
little one was in such a hurry that
he forgot to take off his pyjamas.

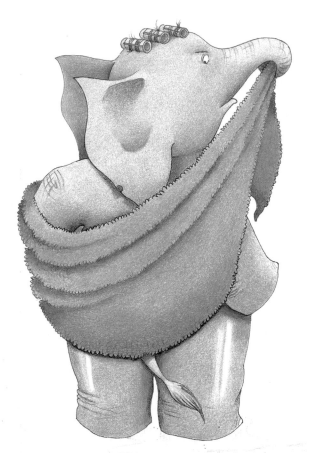

Mrs Large got out. She dried herself, put on her dressing-gown and headed for the door.

'Where are you going *now*, Mum?' asked Laura.

'To the kitchen,' said Mrs Large.

'Why?' asked Lester.

'Because I want five minutes' peace from *you* lot,' said Mrs Large. 'That's why.'

And off she went downstairs, where she had three minutes and forty-five seconds of peace before they all came to join her.

MORE WALKER PAPERBACKS

LEARNING FOR FUN
The Pre-School Years

Shirley Hughes
Nursery Collection

NOISY

COLOURS

BATHWATER'S HOT

ALL SHAPES AND SIZES

TWO SHOES, NEW SHOES

WHEN WE WENT TO THE PARK

John Burningham
Concept Books

COLOURS   ALPHABET

OPPOSITES   NUMBERS

Tony Wells   Puzzle Books

PUZZLE DOUBLES

ALLSORTS

FIRST READERS

Allan Ahlberg
& Colin McNaughton
Red Nose Readers

MAKE A FACE   SO CAN I

BIG BAD PIG   BEAR'S BIRTHDAY

SHIRLEY'S SHOPS   PUSH THE DOG

TELL US A STORY   ONE, TWO, FLEA!

PICTURE BOOKS
For The Very Young

Helen Oxenbury
First Picture Books

PLAYSCHOOL   EATING OUT

THE DRIVE   OUR DOG

THE CHECK-UP   THE VISITOR

THE BIRTHDAY PARTY

GRAN AND GRANDPA

THE DANCING CLASS

Pam Zinnemann-Hope
& Kady MacDonald Denton
The Ned Books

TIME FOR BED NED

LET'S PLAY BALL NED

FIND YOUR COAT NED

LET'S GO SHOPPING NED

Niki Daly Storytime

LOOK AT ME!

JUST LIKE ARCHIE

MONSTERS ARE LIKE THAT

Sarah Hayes & Helen Craig

THIS IS THE BEAR

Sarah Hayes & Jan Ormerod

HAPPY CHRISTMAS, GEMMA

PICTURE BOOKS
For 4 to 6-Year-Olds

Sarah Hayes
The Walker Fairy Tale Library

BOOKS ONE TO SIX

Six collections of favourite stories

Helen Craig
Susie and Alfred

THE NIGHT OF THE PAPER BAG MONSTERS

Philippe Dupasquier

ROBERT THE GREAT

Jane Asher & Gerald Scarfe
The Moppy Stories

MOPPY IS HAPPY   MOPPY IS ANGRY